The Sapiosexual Submissive and Her Cuckquean Fantasy

The Sapiosexual Submissive, Volume 2

Ronda DeMure

Published by Haines Communications, 2024.

Also by Ronda DeMure

The Sapiosexual Submissive
The Sapiosexual Submissive: An Erotic Romance
The Sapiosexual Submissive and Her Cuckquean Fantasy

Standalone
Lick Of The Irish: Red's Journey

Watch for more at https://submissionanddominance.com.

Table of Contents

1. Rachel 1

2. Cuckquean... 7

3. Voyeur.. 13

4. Not a Lesbian 21

5. Domme.. 25

6. Threesome.. 33

7. Goodbye... 37

8. Resolution.. 43

"Two separate beings, in different circumstances, face to face in freedom and seeking justification of their existence through one another, will always live an adventure full of risk and promise." — Simone de Beauvoir, The Second Sex

The Sapiosexual Submissive and Her Cuckquean Fantasy

by Ronda DeMure

1. Rachel

LYDIA WAS SEATED AT a table having lunch with her friend, Rachel, her fingers absently tracing the line of her jaw as she recounted her latest rendezvous with Duncan. Rachel, leaned in with an eager expression, her eyes sparkling with curiosity and a hint of arousal. The restaurant was not busy and there were no other people in earshot, but even so Lydia's voice grew hushed. "He's so attuned to my body," she whispered, her cheeks flushing with the vivid memory. "When he spanks me, it's like he's conducting an orchestra, every stroke building to a crescendo that sends me over the edge."

Rachel's breath caught in her throat at the thought, her own imagination running wild.

"And when he's done," Lydia continued, "his hand slides down to my clit and he makes me cum almost instantly. Then he continues gently caressing it as I come down from the high, and it's... it's like he has total control over me. His touch keeps me so turned on that I'm instantly ready for whatever he wants to do with me next."

Rachel's eyes widened, her own hand subconsciously moving to her lap, where she began to squeeze her thighs together. "Would you... would you mind asking him to spank me?" Rachel's voice was barely a murmur, her eyes searching Lydia's for any sign of judgment.

Lydia felt a jolt of excitement at Rachel's request. It was unexpected, yet the thought of sharing this intimate experience with her friend sent a thrill through her body. Rachel's curiosity had clearly been piqued by the vivid description of her encounters with Duncan. For a moment, she felt a twinge of possessiveness, but then she remembered the way Duncan's gaze had often lingered on Rachel during their intellectual debates, the way Rachel's wit and passion mirrored her own.

"I'll talk to him about it, see if he might be interested," Lydia told her friend, her voice low and filled with a hint of mischief. "But you should know, it's not just about the spanking. There's something... intense between us. It's like our minds connect in a way that makes the physical part even more potent."

Rachel nodded, her eyes glazed over with anticipation.

That evening, Lydia approached Duncan with Rachel's request. He studied her for a moment, his gaze thoughtful before he spoke. "If it's what you want, I'm more than happy to oblige," he warned. "But remember, this is our dynamic. It's not a game or a performance." Secretly, he was thrilled with Lydia's request; Rachel was a very attractive woman. Of greater interest, however, was the potential that this encounter could develop into a threesome with Lydia and another woman; a desire he had not quite known how to bring up.

Lydia nodded, her heart racing at the idea of watching someone else experience what she had grown to crave. She had always harbored a voyeuristic streak, but her outlet had always been online.

The night of the arranged encounter, Rachel arrived at Duncan's house dressed in a simple floral sun dress that hugged her curves and revealed just enough skin to tease at what lay beneath. Duncan greeted her with a friendly hug and a knowing smile that sent a shiver down Rachel's spine. The air was charged with anticipation as they settled into the living room. Duncan directed Lydia and Rachel to sit side by side on the couch as he served them each a glass of mead, and he sat in an easy chair opposite.

"I think we should stand up," Lydia said to Rachel as they finished their wine. "I told Duncan that you have nice legs," Lydia continued, her voice dripping with playfulness. Rachel felt her face heat up as Lydia stood behind her, facing Duncan, and reached for the hem of her dress. She slowly began to pull it up, the fabric gliding over Rachel's smooth, bare legs. Rachel gasped as she felt her friend's hand brush against her thighs.

Duncan leaned back, thoroughly enjoying watching Lydia reveal Rachel's body for him, his gaze intense and hungry.

Rachel leaned into Lydia, her head tilted back and her breath growing shallower with each inch of skin revealed. When the dress was almost to her waist, Lydia's hand slipped under the fabric, caressing the inside of Rachel's right thigh as she met Duncan's gaze with a mischievous smile. Rachel's legs quivered as she felt the warmth of Lydia's breath against her skin.

With a gentle tug, Lydia pulled Rachel's dress up even higher, fully revealing her black panties. Rachel's heart pounded in her chest, her breasts rising and falling with each ragged breath. The fabric was sheer and damp with her arousal. Duncan's eyes grew darker, his pupils dilating as he took in the sight. Lydia's hand traveled higher, brushing against Rachel's breasts in a way that was both casual and intimate. Rachel bit her lower lip while instinctively raising her arms as the fabric of her dress was pulled up and over her head, leaving her in nothing but the scanty underwear.

Now fully exposed, Rachel felt a rush of vulnerability, but also a powerful surge of desire. Lydia stepped back, admiring her handiwork, while Duncan's eyes scanned Rachel's body with an intensity that made her knees weak. He stood, moving closer, his hands reaching out to trace the lines of Rachel's torso, his touch firm but tender. Rachel shivered, her nipples stiffening under his gaze. This was it, she thought to herself. The moment she had fantasized about. The moment when she would truly know if this was what she wanted.

Duncan stood behind Rachel and whispered in her ear, his breath hot against her skin. "Ready?"

Rachel nodded, her voice barely a whisper.

Duncan slid his hands down her arms as he sat on the couch, then suddenly pulled Rachel over his knee. Rachel's heart hammered in her chest as she felt the firmness of his thighs beneath her, his left hand resting gently between her shoulders. He began with light, teasing taps, each one sending a jolt of pleasure through her body. Rachel felt herself relaxing into the sensation, the anticipation of what was to come building within her.

Sensing Rachel's growing comfort, Duncan's spanks grew firmer, more deliberate. Rachel's gasps grew louder with each slap and her body began to tense and squirm. Yet, she found herself craving more, her mind racing with the excitement of being dominated by this man she had admired from afar. As if reading her thoughts, Duncan slid her panties down, revealing her bottom to his view. The coolness of the air on her now naked ass was a stark contrast to the heat building between her legs.

He resumed the spanking, this time with a newfound force that made Rachel's body jolt with every hit.

Rachel's breathing grew ragged as the pain melded into pleasure, her body responding in a way she had never experienced before. Duncan's hand was a blur, each smack resonating through her, pushing her closer and closer to the edge that she had heard Lydia speak so excitedly about. She could feel the wetness between her legs, her arousal soaking Duncan's trousers beneath her.

Duncan then paused for a moment, and slid his hand between her legs. Rachel felt the warmth of his fingertips brushing against her clitoris. A guttural moan escaped her lips, her body begging for more, as Duncan's hand liberally explored her wetness, then soothingly massaged her moisture into her bottom cheeks.

The next set of spanks were delivered with precision, each one hitting with a firmness that made Rachel's eyes water. Yet she didn't want it to stop. Her breath faltered, her body arched, and she felt herself teetering on the brink of something incredible.

Duncan's hand on her neck kept her in place, his grip firm but reassuring. Rachel's eyes closed tightly as she surrendered to the sensations, her mind a whirlwind of pleasure and pain. The room was filled with the sound of skin meeting skin, punctuated by her whimpers and the occasional gasp for breath.

After the final spank landed, Duncan once again slid his had to Rachel's pussy. No sooner had two fingertips alighted on her clitoris when her body convulsed into orgasm. Her back arched, pushing her breasts against Duncan's thigh, and she let out an exuberant scream. He waited, his hand still on her neck, for her to come down from the intense high before gently helping her to stand.

Rachel's legs were wobbly, her body a live wire of sensation, but she couldn't help the smile that spread across her face as she looked up at Lydia, who was watching the scene with a knowing smile.

"How was it?" Lydia asked, her voice gentle and curious. Rachel could only nod, unable to form coherent words. Duncan's touch had been everything she had hoped for and more. The way he had read her body, somehow knowing exactly how much she could handle, had pushed her to new heights of pleasure was unlike anything she had ever experienced. The line between pain and pleasure had blurred into something exquisite and addictive.

Lydia stepped forward, wrapping Rachel in a warm embrace. "Welcome to our world," she whispered in Rachel's ear. Rachel felt a sense of belonging, her body still humming from the aftershocks of her climax. As they pulled apart, Rachel couldn't help but feel a deep connection to the couple she had once only admired from a distance. This was more than just a sexual encounter; it was an invitation into an intimate dance of dominance and submission that she had never dreamed she would be a part of.

The rest of the evening passed in a blur of conversation, laughter, and subtle touches that spoke volumes of the new bond formed between the three of them. Rachel felt a thrill of excitement at the thought of where this might lead. As they sat in the dimly lit room, the sound of classical music playing softly in the background, she began to hope that this was just the beginning of something more.

2. Cuckquean

AFTER RACHEL HAD LEFT, her cheeks still flushed and her step a little unsteady from the evening's events, Lydia and Duncan sat down to a quiet dinner. Lydia was unable to contain her curiosity, finally voicing what had been on her mind since Rachel's departure. "Is it weird that I enjoyed watching you with Rachel?" she asked, her eyes searching Duncan's for any sign of displeasure.

Duncan took a sip of his wine and smiled. "No, not at all," he said, his voice low and reassuring. "Your enjoyment is not only natural, but it's also a testament to your openness and authenticity. It's a concept known as cuckqueaning, where a woman derives pleasure from seeing her partner with another. It's a form of voyeurism, but it also speaks to the depth of connection in our relationship." He reached across the table to take her hand, his thumb gently stroking the back of her knuckles.

"But isn't it... wrong?" Lydia's voice was small, her eyes searching his for understanding.

Duncan leaned back in his chair, his expression contemplative. "Only if it's not what you truly desire," he said. "Our desires are a part of who we are, Lydia. If watching Rachel brought you pleasure, then it's as real and valid as any other aspect of our relationship. The important thing is that we communicate, that we explore these desires together, and that we respect each other's boundaries."

Duncan's words settled warmly into Lydia's mind, soothing any lingering doubt. She felt a rush of affection for this man who understood her so deeply, who accepted and encouraged her to embrace her sexuality without judgment. The way he had dominated Rachel had been thrilling to watch, and she knew that she would crave that power exchange again. But she also knew that their shared desires for the cerebral and the artistic was equally important to her. "I simply adore how you're able to give me so much pleasure, and then hold me and discuss Nietzsche," she said, her voice filled with awe.

Duncan chuckled. "That's what makes us unique," he said. "We have the ability to navigate both the intellectual and the carnally pleasurable with ease. It's a fusion of the mind and body that few truly understand. And with Rachel, it seems we've found someone who shares our appetite for both."

They talked long into the night, sharing thoughts and feelings about their newfound ménage à trois. Lydia felt a sense of liberation, a shedding of societal norms that had once constrained her desires. With Duncan, she had found a partner who not only understood but celebrated her sexuality in all its complexity. The thought of Rachel joining them in their erotic explorations was both exhilarating and terrifying, but she knew that with Duncan in control that everything would be fine.

As they moved to the bedroom, their bodies entwined and their minds still racing with the excitement of the evening, Lydia felt the beginnings of a new chapter in their relationship unfold. The lines between pain and pleasure, between voyeurism and intimacy, had blurred in the most beautiful way possible. And she knew that with Duncan, she would be able to continue to explore those boundaries, pushing ever further into the realms of desire and understanding.

A FEW DAYS LATER, RACHEL and Lydia found themselves sitting across from each other in a different restaurant, their conversation a mix of small talk and the unspoken tension of their shared secret. Rachel's eyes darted to the side every so often, her thoughts clearly elsewhere, and Lydia felt her own heart racing in anticipation of what was to come. They had agreed to meet for lunch to discuss the possibility of taking their encounter to the next level, but neither of them quite knew how to broach the subject. Finally, Rachel took a deep breath, setting down her fork with a clink against the plate. "I can't stop thinking about it," she confessed, her voice low and shaky. "The way he... the way you both... I've never felt anything so intense."

Lydia nodded, her own appetite suddenly forgotten. She reached across the table, her hand finding Rachel's. "I know," she said softly. "It's like we've unlocked something within us, something we never knew we needed." Rachel's hand was warm and slightly trembling, a testament to the emotional turmoil she was feeling.

"But what if it's not just about the spanking?" Rachel asked, her voice barely audible. "What if... I mean, what if I want more?"

Lydia's heart skipped a beat, her thoughts racing. She had been considering this very question, the thought of watching Duncan claim Rachel in the same way he claimed her was both thrilling and terrifying. "More?" she prompted, her voice a whisper.

Rachel's looked directly into her friend's eyes, looking for reassurance. "I don't know," she admitted. "But I can't get the image out of my head. I want to explore this... this... whatever this is, with the two of you."

Lydia felt a surge of arousal at Rachel's admission. She knew that Duncan would be thrilled, that he would revel in the idea of pleasing and dominating Rachel. But she also knew that this would be a very delicate scenario, one that would require deep trust and open communication above all else. "We should talk to Duncan," she finally said, her voice calm and steady. "Make sure we're all on the same page. This isn't something to be taken lightly."

Rachel nodded, her eyes wide and hopeful.

As they sat there, their food growing cold, Lydia couldn't help but wonder where this would lead. Would Rachel become a regular participant in their erotic escapades, a third in their intimate dance? Or was this merely a fleeting curiosity, a moment of shared passion that would fade with time?

Their conversation grew more heated, their words continuing to dance around the edges of what they truly desired. Rachel spoke of her fantasies, her voice filled with a hunger that Lydia recognized all too well. And Lydia, in turn, shared her own thoughts, her own desires, her own fears. They talked of the erotic balance between pain and pleasure, the thrill of giving and receiving, the power of submission and the responsibility of dominance.

With each shared glance and whispered confession, Lydia felt her body responding, her nipples hardening and her pulse quickening. Rachel's cheeks were flushed, her eyes bright with excitement, and Lydia knew that this was the beginning of something special. Something that would challenge them, excite them, and ultimately, bring their friendship closer together.

They left the restaurant with a newfound sense of purpose, their hearts racing and their heads swimming with thoughts of what was to come. As they parted ways, Rachel leaned in, her voice a seductive purr. "Thank you, Lydia," she murmured. "For everything."

Lydia nodded, a knowing smile playing at the corners of her mouth. "You're welcome," she said. "But I have a suspicion that the real fun is just getting started." With that, she turned and walked away, her mind racing with visions of Rachel's bare ass, Duncan's firm hand, and the sweet symphony of pleasure that awaited them all.

3. Voyeur

THAT EVENING, WHEN Lydia and Duncan were alone, she broached the subject with him, her voice a seductive whisper in the dark. "Rachel wants more," she said, her eyes gleaming with excitement. Duncan's breath caught in his throat, his body responding to the anticipation of what that "more" might entail.

"Does she now?" he asked, his tone thoughtful. "But what do you think about that?" His hand slid down her side, tracing the curve of her hip, his thumb lingering on the sensitive skin above her thigh.

"I think... I think it could be amazing," she admitted, her voice trembling slightly. "But I don't want it to ruin the friendship I have with her. Or the relationship that you and I have."

Duncan pulled her closer, his eyes searching hers in the dim light. "We're all adults," he said. "And we are discussing this because it is something that you want. We'll set boundaries, communicate, and make sure everyone is comfortable. If it feels right, we'll explore and see where it leads. If not, we'll stop."

Lydia nodded, Duncan's words lifting a weight from her shoulders. The thought of Rachel desiring the same intense pleasure she experienced with Duncan was both thrilling and a little intimidating. But, as long as Duncan was willing to go along with it... she smiled. Of course he would be willing.

While Duncan had kept the conversation about including Rachel as something he was willing to do for Lydia, the reality was he was incredibly aroused by the idea. Lydia was bringing another woman into their relationship without his ever having to bring up the fact that he wanted a threesome with her.

THE NEXT TIME RACHEL visited, the three of them sat in Duncan's living room together, sipping mead and discussing the latest exhibit at the museum as a means to relax. Lydia had arranged for both of the women to be wearing short, pleated skirts and blouses, with panties but no bra underneath. Rachel seemed anxious and her eyes kept darting between Lydia and Duncan. Lydia smiled as she watched Duncan hungrily gazing at her.

Finally, Rachel took a deep breath and spoke. "Lydia told me that you enjoyed our last encounter," she said to Duncan, her voice a little shaky. "And I, I wanted to know if we could do more this time?"

Duncan leaned back in his chair, his eyes never leaving Rachel's. "What do you have in mind?" he asked, his voice a low rumble. Rachel's cheeks flushed, but she held his gaze, a spark of determination in her eyes. "I want to feel... everything," she said. "I want to experience what Lydia has with you. The spanking was just the beginning."

Lydia felt a thrill run through her at Rachel's words. She knew that Rachel was brave to admit her desires, and she admired her for it. And she couldn't help but feel a sense of pride that her friend was willing to explore this side of herself with them.

Duncan studied Rachel for a moment, then stood up and sat on the couch next to her. He placed his hand on Rachel's knee. "You're sure?" he asked, his voice thick with lust.

Rachel nodded, her breath quickening.

Duncan slid his hand under Rachel's skirt, watching her eyes as he slowly caressed the inside of her right thigh.

Rachel's breath grew heavier and she parted her legs slightly. Lydia watched, her own desire building, as Duncan then leaned in and claimed Rachel's mouth in a kiss that was both tender and demanding. Rachel melted into him, her body arching towards his, and Lydia felt a sudden surge of arousal. This is it, she thought. The moment when the lines between friendship and desire would blur into something new and exciting. And she knew, deep down, that she was ready for whatever came next.

Duncan's hand slid up Rachel's thigh, pushing her skirt higher, while Lydia watched, her eyes dark with desire. Duncan's hand reached Rachel's panties, tracing the edge of the fabric with a feather-light touch that had Rachel's hips bucking towards him. He then slid his hand up across her blouse and began to unbutton it, pulled it open, and fondled her firm breasts.

Lydia initially felt a twinge of something akin to jealousy, but it was quickly overridden by the intense arousal that flooded her body as she watched Duncan kissing and caressing her friend, while Rachel sat compliantly with her blouse open, her skirt up and her legs spread. The sight of Rachel, so wanton and willing, was almost too much to bear. Lydia's own pussy throbbed with need, her body begging for release. She watched as Duncan's fingers deftly took each of Rachel's nipples between his thumb and forefinger and teased them to arousal. Rachel's skin was flushed, her eyes glazed with lust, and Lydia felt a thrill of excitement at being the one to introduce her friend to this world of sensual pleasure.

Duncan's hand slid down Rachel's body, moving to trace the damp fabric of her panties. Rachel gasped, her hips jerking as his thumb grazed her clitoris. Lydia's own hand slipped beneath her skirt, her fingers finding their way to her own wetness.

"I'm going to take your panties off you," Duncan murmured, his voice thick with desire. Rachel nodded, her body trembling with anticipation and her eyes watching Lydia as Duncan slid the garment down her legs an tossing it away.

Duncan slid his right hand over Rachel's exposed pussy, a look of pure hunger etched on his face. He spread Rachel's legs further apart. Her cunt was glistening with arousal.

Lydia felt her own clitoris throb in response, her hand moving faster as she watched Duncan lean in, his breath hot against Rachel's skin.

Two fingers of Duncan's hand slid down to Rachel's clitoris, teasing the sensitive bundle of nerves. Rachel's cry of pleasure was music to Lydia's ears, increasing the desire that echoed in her own body. Rachel's hips rocked as her lips continued to be pushed against Duncan's, her hands grasping at his shoulders as she sought more of his touch.

Lydia continued to watch, her breath coming in shallow pants, as Rachel's body began to tense. She knew that look, had felt it countless times before. Rachel was on the edge, her orgasm building like a crescendo within her. And just when Rachel's climax seemed inevitable, Duncan's mouth pulled away to allow Rachel to gasp loudly as she trembled in orgasm. He enveloped

Rachel in his arms to hold her steady and looked up at Lydia, his eyes gleaming with mischief. "My turn now?" he asked, gesturing to Rachel's trembling form.

Lydia eagerly nodded, her heart racing excitedly as Rachel sank to her knees before Duncan, her hands trembling as she reached for his belt.

The sound of Duncan's zipper seemed to echo through the room. And as Rachel produced his thick, hard cock to their view Lydia's eyes widened, her mouth watering at the sight. Rachel took him in her hand, her touch tentative as she leaned towards it, her lips parting to take him in her mouth.

Duncan groaned, his eyes closing as Rachel began to suck, her tongue swirling and teasing the head of his cock. Lydia watched, her own hand buried in her panties as she stroked herself, the scene before her more erotic than any painting or sculpture they had ever discussed.

Rachel's hand moved to her clitoris and she began to rub it as she took Duncan deeper into her mouth. The sound of Rachel's eagerness was a sweet symphony of pleasure that seemed to resonate throughout the room. Lydia grew more and more excited as Rachel's cheeks hollowed with each bob of her head, her hand moving faster and faster between her legs. Rachel's eyes looked to Lydia, and Lydia, the voyeur, understood that Rachel was taking pleasure not just from Duncan's cock, but from the shared intimacy of the moment.

Duncan's hand tangled in Rachel's hair, guiding her rhythm, his hips bucking slightly as he grew closer to his own release. Rachel's moans of pleasure grew louder, muffled by the cock in her mouth, causing Lydia to slide her panties aside to permit her fingers to delve into her own wetness as she watched her friend take Duncan's length, her own orgasm building in time with Duncan's. The sight of Rachel, her mouth full of Duncan's cock, her eyes glazed with desire, was more than Lydia could handle. With a gasp, she climaxed, her body spasming with pleasure as she watched Rachel's own passion play out before her. Rachel's eyes rolled back in her head as she took Duncan in deeper, her hand moving to stroke her own clit in time with her mouth.

And then, with a guttural groan, Duncan froze, his hands holding Rachel in place while his cock pulsing as he came in her mouth. His hot cum squirted deep into Rachel's throat, but she managed to swallow it. After he released her head, Rachel sat back, her breathing ragged, her body still trembling from her own climax.

Lydia felt a sense of satisfaction watching the scene unfold. The power dynamics of their relationship were clear: Rachel was the eager novice, eager to please and be dominated, while she remained the experienced submissive, watching and learning. But she also knew that their bond was something more, a deep connection that went beyond the physical.

The three of them then sat together on the couch with Rachel between them. She looked up at Lydia, her eyes shining with a newfound understanding, a silent question in her gaze.

"You did well," Lydia murmured, her voice a seductive purr.

Rachel's smile was shy, but it was filled with a sense of accomplishment that only came from exploring one's deepest desires.

The rest of the evening was spent drinking wine, eating cheese, and discussing art and philosophy, their conversation flowing as easily as their earlier exploration of pleasure. But beneath the surface, a new dynamic had been introduced, a current that electrified every touch, every glance, every word. They had crossed a threshold together, and Lydia knew that there was no going back.

4. Not a Lesbian

AS THEY LAY IN BED later that night, Lydia rolled over to face Duncan, her hand idly tracing patterns on his chest. "You know, I've never told anyone this," she began, her voice low and hesitant. "But I've always liked watching porn."

Duncan's eyes opened a fraction, his gaze sharpening with curiosity. "Really?" he asked, his tone casual, though she could see the questioning on his face.

"Yes," she admitted. "And I've noticed that you seem to enjoy certain types of scenes."

He chuckled, a deep rumble that vibrated through her. "Ah, you've been watching what I watch."

"I have," she said, feeling a flush of heat in her cheeks. "The lesbian scenes. The threesomes."

His hand stroked a flop of hair from her face as his eyes searched hers. "Do you like those too?"

"I do," she said, her voice stronger now. "But it's more than just the scenes. It's the power dynamics. The way one person can make another feel so much just with their body."

Duncan's gaze grew intense, his hand sliding up to cup her breast. "You've always had a bit of a dominant streak, haven't you, Lydia?"

"Maybe," she whispered, arching into his touch. "But only in my mind."

He leaned in, his breath warm against her ear. "Tell me, have you ever fantasized about being with a woman?"

Lydia's pulse quickened, her nipples hardening. "Sometimes," she confessed. "But only in a, um, sort of controlling way."

Duncan's thumb began to circle her left nipple, his voice a gentle coax. "What do you mean?"

"I like the idea of, maybe, dominating a woman?" She whispered, her heart racing. "But I'm not a lesbian," she interjected quickly. "I just... Oh, I don't know how to explain it."

Duncan pulled back, looking into her eyes with understanding. "You want to explore," he said, his voice soft. "And that's perfectly fine. It's just another facet of who you are, Lydia."

"But how?" she asked, her voice trembling. "How can I do that without betraying what you and I have?"

Duncan rolled over, his body pressing hers into the mattress, his weight deliciously heavy. "By understanding that your desires, your fantasies, are just that - fantasy. They don't define you in the real world, just like your submissive nature doesn't define you outside of this bedroom." He leaned in, his lips brushing hers in a soft, lingering kiss. "And as your Dominant, I'm here to guide you, to help you navigate those desires. To show you how to take control without losing yourself."

The weight of his body was a comfort, his words a revelation. Lydia felt the last of her inhibitions slipping away as she kissed him back, her hand sliding down to grip his hardening cock. "Show me," she breathed against his lips. "Teach me."

Duncan's eyes darkened with hunger, his hand sliding down to cup her ass. "With pleasure," he murmured, his teeth nipping at her lower lip.

And with that, their world expanded, the boundaries of their relationship stretching to include new realms of pleasure and power. Rachel's introduction into their intimacy had only been the beginning. Now, with Duncan's guidance, Lydia would learn to embrace the depths of her own desires, to become not just the submissive, but a dominant over a woman in her own right. She still had mixed feelings about her own sexuality. While she had no romantic interest in women, she often became aroused at seeing a woman naked. Touching Rachel had excited her even more. Duncan explained that it was not sexuality, but sensuality. Lydia craved sensual delights, and a woman's body was very sensual indeed.

Their connection was not a simple thing. It was a complex tapestry of intellect and passion, of submission and dominance, of pain and pleasure. And as they lay tangled together in the aftermath of their confessions, Lydia knew that with Duncan by her side, she could conquer any fear, explore any desire. Together, they would continue to challenge the norms, to push the boundaries of what was accepted, and to revel in the sensuality of their shared experiences. Their future held a thrilling array of possibilities, and as Lydia felt the heat of Duncan's cock pressing against her, she knew that she was ready to explore them all. After all, it was Duncan who had introduced her to the pleasure of what he was about to do with her, something which before him would have been abhorrent and painful.

Lying with her back to him, he took her wrists in his right hand and held them above her head as his left hand massaged her buttocks, parting them to allow the entrance of the moist head of his cock into her puckered anal entrance. He pushed an inch inside and held still until she was ready, then slowly leaned into her until his pelvis was touching her. He withdrew halfway, then plunged back in again.

She felt his breath on the back of her neck and his teeth nibbling her shoulder as he began to fuck her ass. Faster and faster. Then both of his hands were on her hips, holding her in place, driving her wild. She screamed into orgasm as he rolled her over so she was face down on the bed with him lying on top of her, pinning her down, taking her almost violently until he finally came up her ass.

5. Domme

RACHEL EAGERLY ACCEPTED their invitation to dinner the following Saturday. Lydia had told her that they would both be interacting with her, but she had no idea what that actually meant. Aroused by the mystery, Rachel arrived at Duncan's house wearing a simple black dress with nothing underneath.

Their dinner conversation was filled with a new energy, the air thick with the promise of what was to come. They talked of art and literature, of their shared love of philosophy, but beneath it all was the thrumming beat of their newfound sexual connection. Rachel was quieter than usual, her eyes darting between Duncan and Lydia as if trying to understand the dynamics of what they had in store for her.

As the wine flowed and the candles flickered, the conversation grew more intimate, more personal. Rachel began to open up more, sharing her own fantasies, her own hidden desires, and Lydia found herself drawn to her friend in a way she hadn't anticipated. The intellectual connection they shared was now laced with something more primal, sexual even. Duncan suggested that they adjourn to the couch.

Rachel sat between them, a picture of beauty and desire, her eyes shining with excitement. Duncan's hand slipped under Rachel's dress, and he smiled on the discovery that she was without panties. Rachel gasped, her eyes fluttering shut as his thumb brushed over her clitoris.

Lydia watched, her own arousal growing as Rachel's hips began to rock in time with Duncan's touch. Rachel's body was a canvas of passion, each touch and kiss a stroke that painted her with desire. Duncan's other hand slid around Rachel's waist, pulling her closer to him, and Lydia felt a pang of something new - a fierce, possessive need to claim Rachel for herself.

With trembling hands, Lydia pushed Rachel's dress up, removing it by sliding it over her head and rendering her naked. She reached for Rachel's breasts, her palms cupping the soft mounds as she leaned in to capture one of Rachel's nipples in her mouth. Rachel moaned, arching into the sensation, her body moving in a silent plea for more. The taste of Rachel's skin, the feel of her flesh beneath Lydia's touch, was intoxicating.

Duncan watched. He moved his hand away from Rachel's pussy as Lydia explored the contours of Rachel's body. The sight of Lydia with another woman, the sound of Rachel's moans, was driving him wild with desire.

As Rachel's breath grew shallower, Lydia felt the power surging within her. The way Rachel's body responded to her touch was addictive, a heady rush that she hadn't expected. She wanted to make Rachel cum, wanted to show Duncan that she could be the one in control. Her hand slid down Rachel's stomach, her fingertips teasing the dampness of Rachel's pussy before plunging into the heat between her labia lips. Rachel's hips bucked, her hands grabbing fistfuls of Lydia's hair as she rode the wave of pleasure. Lydia watched Rachel's face, her own climax building as she felt Rachel tighten around her fingers.

And then Rachel was coming, her body convulsing with the force of her orgasm, her cries of pleasure muffled by the couch cushions. Lydia felt the wetness of Rachel's release coat her hand, a tangible reminder of the power she wielded.

The three of them sat there for a moment, panting and sated, before Rachel found her voice, her eyes shining with gratitude and wonder. "I never knew it could be like this," she said, her words filled with awe.

Lydia looked up at Duncan, her heart pounding. "Neither did I," she admitted. "And I want more."

Duncan's smile was filled with pride. "Then we'll give you more," he promised. "We'll explore every facet of your sexuality, together."

Rachel leaned back against the couch, her body still trembling from the intensity of her climax, and Duncan told Lydia to stand up. "Take your clothes off," he ordered, his voice firm and commanding.

Rachel watched, her eyes wide with excitement as Lydia obeyed, her clothes falling to the floor as she stripped in front of them. Rachel felt a thrill at the sight of Lydia's naked body, so vulnerable and exposed before them.

Lydia's eyes met Rachel's, a silent challenge, and Rachel felt the heat rising in her cheeks as she took in the beauty of her friend's body. The way her breasts rose and fell with each breath, the curve of her waist, the softness of her thighs. Rachel had never seen her friend look so alluring.

"Now, Rachel," Duncan said, his hand on Rachel's shoulder, guiding her to her knees. "It's your turn to serve."

Rachel swallowed hard, her heart racing as she knelt before Lydia, her gaze dropping to the wetness glistening between Lydia's legs.

Duncan placed his hand on Rachel's head, his fingers tangling in her hair. "You're going to lick Lydia," he instructed, his voice a low growl as he guided her forward.

Rachel leaned in, her mouth watering as she breathed in the scent of Lydia's arousal. Her first kiss was tentative, a soft press of her lips against Lydia's clitoris that made the woman before her gasp. Rachel felt a thrill that coursed through her veins as she realized that she could bring Lydia to the edge of pleasure just as she had previously done for Duncan. With renewed confidence, Rachel began to lick and suck, her tongue tracing patterns across Lydia's cunt, her teeth grazing the sensitive flesh.

Lydia's thighs tensed and her hands came to rest on Rachel's shoulders, guiding her movements. Rachel's eyes never left Lydia's, watching the play of emotions on her face as she brought her closer and closer to climax.

Duncan's hand tightened in Rachel's hair, his breathing growing heavier as he watched the scene unfold. Rachel felt the pressure build, the intensity of Lydia's desire a palpable force in the room. And when Lydia finally came, her body shaking with the force of her orgasm, Rachel felt a sense of triumph, her own arousal reaching new heights.

Lydia's legs trembled as Rachel eased back, a soft smile playing on her lips. "Good girl," she murmured, her voice a hoarse whisper.

Rachel looked up, her cheeks flushed and her eyes sparkling with excitement.

"You did well," Duncan also praised Rachel.

Rachel felt a warmth spread through her, his approval as potent as any physical touch.

"And now," Duncan told her, his voice thick with lust. "I'm going to enjoy you both."

He stood, pulling Rachel to her feet, and then had her and Lydia sit down, side by side, on the couch. Rachel watched in wonder as Duncan stripped off his own clothes and stood facing them both, his cock standing proudly before them.

"Take me in your mouth," he told Rachel, his voice a gentle command.

Rachel obeyed, her heart racing as she took his length into her mouth.

With Rachel already servicing his cock, Duncan's attention shifted to Lydia. He put his hand on the back of Lydia's head and pushed her forward, guiding her closer until her face was next to Rachel's.

Rachel looked up, her eyes wide with excitement as Duncan's shaft slipped from her mouth and was replaced by Lydia's eager lips. Rachel took the moment to kiss and lick at the base of his cock, her tongue tracing the sensitive veins that pulsed with his desire.

The two women took turns, their lips and tongues worshiping his length. Duncan groaned in pleasure, his hips moving in a slow, steady rhythm as he fed his cock to Rachel, then Lydia, then Rachel again. Each time he pulled out of one mouth, the other was there to greet him, a wet, warm cavern eager for his return. Rachel watched as Lydia's cheeks hollowed with the effort of deep-throating him, the way her eyes rolled back in pleasure. Rachel felt a surge of desire, not just for the man before them, but for the woman who was sharing this moment with her.

Their rhythm grew faster, the sounds of wet suction and muffled moans filling the room. Lydia's hand slipped to Rachel's breast, her thumb massaging Rachel's nipple as she took her turn, and Rachel couldn't help but arch into the touch. The sensation of Lydia's hand on her, the taste of Duncan in her mouth, was an intoxicating mix of pleasure and submission.

Duncan's breath grew ragged, his hips jerking with the effort of holding back his climax. He pulled out of Lydia's mouth, his hand tangling in Rachel's hair as he brought her back to his cock. Rachel felt the tension in his body, the way he was holding back for them. She redoubled her efforts, her mouth moving faster, her tongue swirling around his head, her teeth grazing just enough to make him gasp.

Lydia's hand slid down to Rachel's pussy, her fingers teasing Rachel's clitoris as Rachel continued to suck Duncan off. The pressure inside Rachel was building, her hips moving in time with Lydia's touch.

Duncan's hand tightened on Rachel's head, and Rachel knew what was coming. She braced herself, her mouth still full of him, as Lydia's hand began to pump faster and faster. Rachel's eyes watered with the effort of holding back, her mouth moving in a blur as she felt her own orgasm approaching. And just as she thought she couldn't take anymore, Duncan's hand froze in her hair, and Rachel felt the first hot spurt of his cum hit the back of her throat. She swallowed greedily, the taste of him mixing with the pleasure that was already coursing through her body.

As Rachel's orgasm washed over her, Duncan pulled out of her mouth, his cock still pulsing with the aftershocks of his release. Rachel collapsed against Lydia, the two of them panting and laughing, their bodies tangled together in a mess of limbs and desire.

6. Threesome

DUNCAN LOOKED DOWN at Lydia and Rachel as they lay together on the couch, his expression one of pure satisfaction. "You both did so well," he murmured, his hand stroking Rachel's cheek.

Rachel felt a warmth spread through her, a sense of belonging at being included in his and Lydia's fantasy world. "Thank you," she whispered, looking up at Duncan.

He sat down next to her, cupped Rachel's chin, and tilted her face up to his. His eyes searched hers, looking for any sign of concern, but all he saw was desire. He leaned forward and gave her a kiss, then turned to Lydia, his hand sliding down Rachel's body to cup her breast. "You're both so beautiful," he murmured, his finger and thumb squeezing Rachel's nipple. Lydia watched, smiling, her eyes filling with lust as Rachel's body responded to the gentle torment.

"I want to watch you and Lydia," Rachel whispered, her voice hoarse with desire. "I want to see how you make her scream."

Duncan's eyes lit up with a wicked glint. "As you wish," he said, his hand leaving Rachel's breast to guide her to the chair opposite the couch. Rachel sat, her legs spread wide, her eyes now focusing on Lydia's body.

Lydia's pulse raced as Duncan turned his full attention to her. He pushed her gently down onto the couch, his body moving to cover hers. Rachel watched as her hand slid down her stomach to stroke her clitoris, while Duncan kissed and nibbled Lydia's body. His tongue traced the line of Lydia's collarbone, then moved to her breasts, his teeth teasing the sensitive flesh until she was moaning.

Rachel felt her own arousal spike as she watched Duncan's hand move down Lydia's stomach and reaching for her pussy. Rachel's eyes were glued to the sight as Lydia's moans grew louder, her hands gripping the fabric of the couch as Duncan's fingers worked their magic. She watched with delight how Lydia's thighs trembled with the effort to stay still. She was almost there when Duncan moved to spread Lydia's legs apart and positioned his engorged cock between them, teasing her labia lips with the glistening purple head.

Lydia arched her body off the couch in an attempt to coax Duncan inside her, but he held her legs up and apart which deprived her of any control. Then, suddenly, he thrust himself all the way inside her. She came instantly, her screams of pleasure echoing through the room.

Rachel felt warmth spread through her, her own orgasm close. Her hand moved faster and faster as she chased the feeling that was building inside her.

As Lydia's cries subsided, Rachel looked up to find Duncan watching her. "Come here," he said in an authoritative voice that sent a shiver down Rachel's spine. Rachel stood, her legs wobbly with desire, and made her way to the couch, her heart racing with anticipation of what Duncan was going to make her do.

Duncan took her hand, his cock still embedded in Lydia's cunt, and Rachel realized that what Duncan wanted was what she had been waiting for. At his direction, she straddled Lydia's face, her pussy already wet and ready, and lowered herself onto her friend's mouth. The feeling of Lydia's tongue was exquisite, and she rocked back and forth against it.

Duncan continued his fucking of Lydia, while Lydia frantically licked Rachel. He then leaned forward, kissed Rachel, and pulled her head down toward Lydia's abdomen. He withdrew his cock from Lydia, forced it between Rachel's parted lips, and continued to pump. On the third thrust he exploded into Rachel's mouth.

Duncan then slid out and pushed Rachel's mouth between Lydia's legs, ordering her to lick. He watched Rachel's tongue slide out obediently to taste Lydia, her eyes closing in bliss as she felt the warm, wet embrace of Lydia's pussy. Lydia's hips bucked upward, her body responding instinctively, and Rachel moaned with excitement.

The two women rocked together in a silent rhythm, each lost in the pleasure of giving and receiving oral pleasure. Duncan sat back on the chair opposite, his hand stroking his cock, watching as these two women became one. Rachel's eyes were closed tight, her mouth a perfect O around Lydia's clitoris, and Lydia's eyes were looking over at him, a silent plea for his guidance, his approval.

Rachel's movements grew more frantic, her hips grinding into Lydia's face as she neared climax. Lydia's mouth moved faster, her own body responding to Rachel's building pleasure, her tongue licking and swirling until Rachel's legs began to tremble. She felt the first ripple of her orgasm begin, her body tightening around Lydia's face as she rode out the waves of pleasure. Lydia's mouth was relentless, her tongue never ceasing its movements as Rachel's body convulsed with each spasm of ecstasy.

And then Rachel was coming, her hips bucking as she cried out, her orgasm as waves of pleasure that seemed to go on forever. Lydia drank from her greedily, her own desire for release growing stronger with each shudder that passed through Rachel's body. Rachel felt herself being pushed to the edge, her own climax building, the pressure in her clitoris becoming unbearable.

With a final, desperate lick, Rachel felt Lydia's body tense beneath her, her own orgasm crashing over her like a wave. Rachel's mouth filled with Lydia's sweetness, and she swallowed, her own body shaking with the power of her release.

When the tremors had subsided, Rachel lifted her head, her cheeks flushed and her eyes glazed with satisfaction. Lydia's body was limp, her chest heaving with the effort of her climax. Rachel looked up at Duncan, her eyes filled with a mix of awe and desire.

"That was... amazing," Rachel managed to say, her voice a hoarse whisper. She stayed with them until the early morning before leaving for home, wonderfully satiated.

Duncan wrapped his arms around Lydia. "Tell me," he said. "How do you like having a woman make you cum with her tongue?"

"It was wonderful." Lydia held onto him with her face nestled in the nape of his neck. "And you enjoyed watching, didn't you?"

"I did."

7. Goodbye

THE NEXT DAY, SUNDAY morning, Duncan woke up earlier than usual, and decided to make breakfast. Soon the aroma of freshly brewed coffee and sizzling bacon filled the kitchen. He knew Lydia liked to sleep in, and he hoped the meal would be a comforting start to the day for her after their wonderful night of erotic pleasure. However, as he placed the steaming plates on the dining table, he was aware of tension in the air. Lydia was unusually quiet, and he could see the conflict playing out in her expressive eyes. In the harsh light of day, the complexities of their relationship were coming into focus for her. Being with Rachel had stirred a cocktail of emotions in Lydia, and Duncan knew that jealousy was one of the ingredients. He approached her gently, setting her plate down and placing a soft kiss on her forehead. "What's on your mind, Lydia?" He asked with genuine concern

Lydia took a deep breath, her eyes lingering on the plate before her. "I can't stop thinking about Rachel," she admitted, her voice tight. "And how much pleasure you gave her."

Duncan's hand found hers, giving it a gentle squeeze. "I know you enjoyed watching," he said, his voice soothing. "But if it's causing an issue for you then we need to talk about it."

"It's not the watching," Lydia clarified, her eyes searching his. "It's just that I want you to feel the same way she does. To be consumed by pleasure, to lose yourself in it."

Duncan leaned back in his chair, his thumb tracing idle circles on her hand. "I did, I do," he assured her. "But in a different way. Watching you two together was intoxicating for me, too."

He could see the doubt in her eyes, the way her mind was racing. "But it's not enough," she whispered. "I want to feel it, to be the one to give you that kind of pleasure."

He leaned in closer, his gaze intense. "You do," he said, his voice low and filled with meaning. "Every time you submit to me, every time you allow me to explore your body, to push you to the brink, I realize that pleasure."

The words hung in the air, and for a moment, Lydia's expression softened. But the doubt remained. It was as if a shadow were hovering over her. Duncan knew that this conversation was far from over. As they ate, Duncan could feel Lydia's grasp on the situation weakening. Her eyes looked up to meet his. "I just don't want to lose what we have," she said, her voice barely audible.

Duncan took a deep breath. "You won't," he promised, his thumb brushing away a stray tear from Lydia's cheek. "This is just another facet of who we are. We'll navigate it together, just like everything else."

The conversation that followed was filled with passion and vulnerability and served to reassure Lydia of the depth of their connection. By they were finishing their breakfast, they were discussing having Rachel over again, and this time for a proper threesome.

Lydia was extremely aroused at the thought of watching her friend being properly fucked by Duncan and told him how much she would like to see that. The future was indeed uncertain, but in that moment she knew that she should be able to handle any challenge that came her way. Her cuckquean persona had overridden her feelings of jealousy.

Duncan took Lydia's hand, leading her to the bedroom where he lay her down on the soft, inviting sheets. "We'll take this slow," he assured her, his voice a gentle rumble in the quiet room. "We'll talk through everything."

WHEN RACHEL ARRIVED the following Saturday evening, the anticipation in the air was electric. Lydia's heart raced with both excitement and a hint of trepidation. Rachel looked stunning, her eyes gleaming with the same hunger that Duncan had seen in Lydia's earlier that week. But it was Rachel's openness, her willingness to submit to both of them, that truly set Lydia's pulse racing.

The three of them moved together with a grace that seemed almost choreographed, their bodies melding into a single unit of desire and need. Rachel's soft moans filled the air as Lydia kissed her, their tongues dancing together as Duncan's hands explored Rachel's body. Lydia felt the heat building in her own core, the sight of Duncan's fingers disappearing into Rachel's wetness driving her wild with lust.

Duncan looked at Lydia, his gaze questioning, and she nodded, her own desire burning brighter than ever before. Rachel's eyes widened with excitement as Duncan positioned himself between her legs, his cock standing proud and ready. Rachel reached out, her hand brushing over Lydia's breasts as she watched in awe.

The sensation of Duncan's cock sliding into Rachel sent shivers down her spine. And as he began to move, Rachel could feel Lydia's eyes on her, watching her every reaction. Neither did Rachel's eyes leave Lydia's, the connection between them growing stronger with each thrust that Duncan pumped into her,

Lydia's hand slid down her own body, her fingers finding her clitoris as she watched Rachel's face contort with pleasure. The sight of Duncan's cock disappearing into Rachel's pussy was a strange mix of arousal and something else, something deeper that she couldn't quite put her finger on.

But as Rachel's moans grew louder, as her body began to tremble with the beginnings of an orgasm, Lydia felt a surge of something she hadn't anticipated. Jealousy, yes, but also a fierce possessiveness. Her hand moved faster, her body was craving the same release that Rachel was experiencing.

And then Rachel came. Her body arched off the bed as Duncan's cock filled her completely. Lydia felt the first twinges of her own climax, her hand moving faster and faster as Rachel's cries grew more insistent. But Lydia also felt a strange mix of emotions as she watched Rachel's orgasm play out. She was thrilled, of course, to have shared in this moment of passion with her friend. But there was something else, something that whispered in the back of her mind, a question that she couldn't quite silence. Why did Duncan want this? Why would he want to be inside someone else when he had her? The thrill of sharing Duncan, of watching him with another woman, was what she had thought she wanted, but she hadn't anticipated her irrational feelings to be so strong.

THE NEXT DAY, AS SHE sat at her desk, the sun streaming through the window and illuminating the screen of her laptop, Lydia felt a heaviness in her chest that she couldn't ignore. She typed out an email, her fingers hovering over the keys as she tried to find the right words to convey her tumultuous emotions without sounding clingy or overly dramatic. "Duncan," she began, her heart racing with each syllable. "I need to tell you goodbye."

Her thoughts swirled as she wrote, trying to articulate the jealousy that had woken her in the early hours of the morning. "I don't think I can do this," she admitted. "I thought I could handle it, but the idea of you with Rachel is just too much." The words flowed out of her, a river of inadequacy and doubt that she hadn't realized had been building within her. "I can't help but feel like I'm not enough for you," she confessed. The email was a raw, unfiltered expression of her soul, her deepest fears laid bare for him to see. She hit send with a trembling hand, her eyes blurry with unshed tears.

Duncan read the email with a heavy heart, feeling the weight of her words like a stone in his stomach. But then he became angry. He and Lydia had frequently discussed how their D/s time was when each partner objectifies the other, and each stays in their role. When the playtime was over, then each person was simply reduced to a pile of flesh. This made people generally uninteresting at that point, unless they also had a relationship in the real world. Duncan had made it clear from the beginning that he and Lydia had something unique, that they shared both a fantasy world and a life in the real world. Jealousy can happen easily in the real world, but it should never exist in the fantasy world because it denies the authenticity of being that particular object there. Pure pleasure for its own sake. Lydia had blurred these lines. And furthermore, she had the audacity in feeling entitled to do so. Where was Lydia's authenticity? Duncan had to wonder what her real motivation had been with their relationship. He angrily responded:

"Rachel was just a part of our exploration. A toy, if you will, for us to enjoy in our fantasy world. But your goodbye email has clearly told me that our relationship has run its course."

He clicked send. He knew that words alone would probably make her as angry as he was, but so be it.

8. Resolution

THEN ONE EVENING, ALMOST three months later, Lydia called Duncan. Her voice was small, almost hesitant, and Duncan could hear the vulnerability in her tone. "I'd like to talk," she said. "Can we meet?"

The café where they met was their usual spot, filled with the comforting scent of brewing coffee and the soft murmur of intellectual debates. Lydia was waiting for him when he arrived, her eyes red from crying but her gaze steady. She took a deep breath as he sat down, her hand trembling slightly as she reached for her cup.

"I've been thinking," she began, her voice low. "I know that a threesome is a part of what you desire, a part of your sexuality." She took a sip of her coffee, the liquid burning a path down her throat. "But I don't know if I can share you like that. So my question is, why can't you find another couple of women and just not tell me about it?"

Duncan reached across the table, taking her hand in his. "You're missing the point, Lydia." He shook his head. "I didn't want a generic threesome, I wanted you and I to enjoy a woman together. It was to be something for us to share, something which would enhance our relationship even further. The D/s world and the real world are separate entities. They serve different purposes, fulfill different needs. I thought you understood that. Rachel was just an extension of our play, a way for us to explore something new. But you ruined that. You allowed jealousy, which should only exist in the real world, into our perfect fantasy world and destroyed the purity of it. I told you to never blur the lines between what is fantasy and what is real."

Lydia looked down at their joined hands, the warmth of his touch a stark contrast to the cold realization dawning within her. "I did," she murmured. "I didn't mean to, but watching," she gulped. "Watching you with Rachel. It just, it just changed things for me."

Duncan squeezed her hand gently. "Then you need to decide if you can again separate the two." The intensity of their shared intellectual life was what had initially drawn them together into a real world relationship and he knew that neither of them wanted to lose that. But it would be impossible to have that without the fantasy world they had created together. The fire of their sexual explorations had become equally important. She was his submissive in one world and his friend in the other, and for him it had to be both or nothing.

"If you can accept an occasional threesome as part of our sexual dynamics without letting it infiltrate our real world life," he continued. "Then we have the possibility to resume what we had. Are you able to do that?"

Lydia's heart raced as she searched his eyes, looking for any sign of compromise. But she knew that Duncan was resolute, that his words were the ultimatum she had feared. "I'll try," she whispered, her voice thick with emotion. The café's ambiance faded away as they sat there, their world narrowing to the table between them, the warmth of their hands entwined. "For us, I'll try."

Duncan leaned back in his chair and slowly shook his head. "You need to be certain, Lydia. This isn't a game. Our connection is too strong to be compromised by your jealousy."

Lydia took a deep breath, the weight of his words settling heavily on her. She knew he was right. "I'll work on it," she promised, her voice firm with determination. "I won't let this come between us."

Duncan's smile was tight, a silent acknowledgment of the battle she faced within herself. "I know you will," he said. "Because you're strong, and because you know how wonderful what we have is."

Their continued conversation was delicate, a balancing act between passion and logic. They talked for hours, dissecting their emotions and desires with the precision of philosophers. And as the night grew late, Lydia felt a flicker of hope. Perhaps she could find a way to embrace both sides of their relationship, to cherish the depth of their intellectual bond while also reveling in the intensity of their sexual explorations.

"Let's take it slow," Duncan suggested, his voice a soothing balm to her frazzled nerves. "We will include Rachel on occasion but will recognize that she is just a part of our fantasy times together. We'll communicate, set boundaries, and we shall see where all of this goes."

Lydia nodded, feeling a sense of relief wash over her. "Yes," she said, her voice a whisper. "Let's do this." She looked up with a genuine smile. "I really want to."

THEIR NEXT ENCOUNTER with Rachel began as a tentative one, the air thick with unspoken tension. But as the night progressed, Lydia found herself slipping back into her role with ease, the thrill of the forbidden mixing with the comfort of the familiar. Rachel's cries of pleasure were a siren's song, a reminder of the depth of their connection.

As Rachel's body trembled with the aftershocks of her climax, Lydia watched with a mix of fascination and acceptance. This was their world, their fantasy, and she had found her place within it. She and Rachel were now not only friends but sex partners who were both submissive to Duncan, following his directions as he orchestrated their scenes. While she had enjoyed directing Rachel, she felt more comfortable sharing with Duncan what it was that she wanted and having him tell them both what to do. He would make her fantasies real for her.

The trio continued to explore, their boundaries stretching and morphing with each new experience. The line between pain and pleasure grew thinner, but the line between their real world and their fantasy world would remain firmly intact.

Did you love *The Sapiosexual Submissive and Her Cuckquean Fantasy*? Then you should read *The Sapiosexual Submissive: An Erotic Romance*[1] by Ronda DeMure!

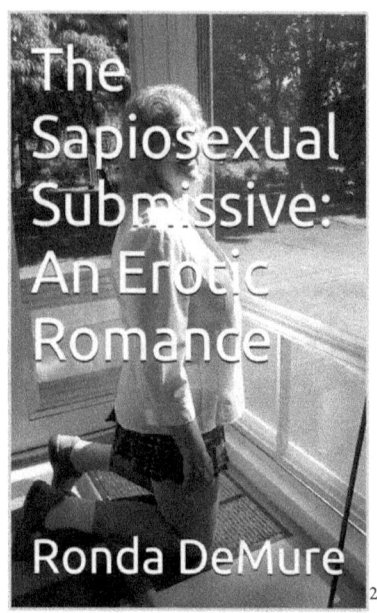

[2]

Single since her divorce years ago, Lydia's life is mostly occupied with business success and she has no wish to marry again, but there is a gnawing void in her life that the conventional world of dating with its superficial conversations and focus on the trivial cannot fill. She requires intelligence, but most of the men she meets are as intellectually unstimulating as the unimaginative sex that goes with them. She therefore decides to take a foray into the world of submission and dominance. She meets Duncan, an experienced dominant who is also mentally compatible with her, and she finds she cannot help but adore him as he engages in her female submissive training. She is aroused by both the physical and the psychological submission and soon relishes the pleasure pain balance which Duncan uses to enter her into subspace.Duncan keeps his world of dominance and submission completely separate from his very visible real world and relegates the people he meets to either one side of his life or the other. Lydia may be his perfect submissive, but she would have to remain in that secret compartment and have no impact on the rest of his life if he is to continue with her. Yet as his growing feelings for his sapiosubmissive become more and more apparent the barrier between his two worlds becomes uncomfortably blurry and he must find a solution. A solution that matches their unique situation: sapiosexuals in a submissive and dominant relationship.

Read more at https://submissionanddominance.com.

Also by Ronda DeMure

The Sapiosexual Submissive
The Sapiosexual Submissive: An Erotic Romance
The Sapiosexual Submissive and Her Cuckquean Fantasy

Standalone
Lick Of The Irish: Red's Journey

Watch for more at https://submissionanddominance.com.